Books in the Animal Ark Pets series

BEN M. BAGLIO

HAMSTER HOTEL

Illustrated by
Paul Howard

Cover Illustration by
Chris Chapman

A
LITTLE APPLE
PAPERBACK

SCHOLASTIC INC.

New York Toronto London Auckland Sydney
Mexico City New Delhi Hong Kong

Special thanks to Sue Welford.
Thanks also to C.J. Hall, B.Vet.Med., M.R.C.V.S., for reviewing
the veterinary material contained in this book.

ISBN 0-439-05161-4

Text copyright © 1996 by Ben M. Baglio.
Illustrations copyright © 1996 by Paul Howard.

24 23 22 21 20 19 18 17 16 15 14   3 4/0

Printed in the U.S.A.   40

First Scholastic trade paperback printing, April 1999

Contents

1

A Visitor at Lilac Cottage

"Mandy Hope, did you hear what I said?" Mrs. Todd was standing right beside Mandy's school desk.

Mandy looked up at her teacher. She had been miles away. Today was the day that her grandmother's friend Mary was bringing her hamster to stay at Lilac Cottage, Mandy's grandparents' house.

Mandy's grandparents were going to look after the hamster for a week while Mary was away on vacation. Mandy just couldn't wait to meet him.

"Oh, sorry, Mrs. Todd," she said. "Er . . . no, I didn't."

"What's the heaviest animal on land in the world, next to the elephant, Mandy?"

The class was having a quiz and it was Mandy's turn to answer a question.

"Oh," Mandy said. "A rhinoceros."

You could ask Mandy anything about animals and she almost always knew the answer.

Mrs. Todd nodded. "Good. Very nice, Mandy!"

Mandy glanced up at the clock. Three o'clock, almost time to go home. Better still, it was vacation. She and her best friend, James Hunter, would have a whole week to spend with the hamster. James was a year younger than Mandy and loved animals almost as much as she did.

James had two pets. A Labrador puppy named Blackie and a cat named Benji. Mandy would have loved to have a pet, too. But her parents were both vets and were too busy looking after other people's animals to have pets of their own.

Mandy wanted to be a vet like her parents one day. She longed to help out with the sick animals at their clinic, Animal Ark, but knew she would have to wait until she was older.

When school had finished, Mandy helped Mrs. Todd take Terry and Jerry, the class gerbils, out to her car. Mrs. Todd was going to care for them at her house during the vacation.

Mandy said good-bye to Mrs. Todd, then ran to meet James who was waiting by the school gate. They always went home together.

"Today's hamster day!" Mandy zipped up her coat against the cold wind.

James pushed his glasses onto the bridge of his nose. "I didn't forget," he said. "When can I come and see him?"

"Mom said I could go straight to Grandma's after school," Mandy said. "You could come with me now if you like."

"Will your grandma mind?" James asked.

"Of course she won't," said Mandy.

"Great!" said James, hurrying to keep up. "Let me just tell my mom where I'm going." He ran on ahead to his house.

"Don't be long," Mandy called. "And you better not bring Blackie this time — he might frighten the hamster."

James disappeared into his house.

Mandy waited for him by the front gate. Suddenly a black nose pushed the back door open and Blackie came running out. James followed soon after.

"Blackie!" James shouted. "Come back."

Blackie threw himself at Mandy, all big paws and wagging tail. Mandy laughed and gave him a cuddle. Blackie rolled over on his back with his legs in the air so Mandy could tickle his tummy.

James caught up with them and grabbed the puppy's collar. "Blackie, *when* will you learn to do as you're told?" He gently shook the puppy and scolded him. "He's learned to open the door," James explained to Mandy.

"So I see." She laughed.

Blackie stood up and began licking her face. Mandy gave him another hug. "You're a very clever dog," she said.

"Yes, he is, but when is he going to behave?" said James.

"Never, by the looks of it." Mandy pushed Blackie gently away. "You'll have to take him to puppy training classes."

"Dad's already taken him," James told her as he hauled Blackie back into the house. "But he caused a riot."

Mandy chuckled. "A riot?"

"Yes. He ran off with the trainer's whistle, stole the treats they were going to have at break time, and got hold of a lady's scarf and tore it to pieces. Dad won't take him again."

"I'm not surprised." Mandy burst out laughing. "One of our vacation jobs will have to be some serious training with Blackie," she said.

James looked sad. "We can try," he said. "But I don't have much hope — he hasn't gotten better since the last time we tried."

Mandy skipped ahead as they made their way across the village green. It was a damp afternoon, with a hint of drizzle in the wind. "Come on, I can't wait to see the hamster!"

Grandpa was busy in the garden of Lilac Cottage, pruning back the shrubs. The sleeves of his old gardening sweater were pushed up to the elbows. There was a wheelbarrow full of twigs and leaves on the path. Mandy pushed past and ran to give him a hug.

"Have you come to see Frisky, the hamster?" Grandpa asked.

"Yep. I've brought James."

"Very good," Grandpa said. "Hello, James. How are you?"

"Fine, thank you, Mr. Hope," James said.

"That's good. Go on in, Grandma's in her study typing some letters."

"Grandma, I'm here!" Mandy called as she and James went in through the back door. The click-clack of Grandma's old-fashioned typewriter came from the other room. "James is with me."

Mandy looked around the kitchen. There was no sign of the hamster. They went into Grandma's study.

"Hello, you two," Grandma said.

Mandy gave her grandma a kiss. "Where is he, Grandma?"

Grandma turned around in her chair and took off her glasses. "If you mean Frisky, I've put him in the spare room. It's nice and light, and warm by the radiator."

"May we go up and see him, please?"

"Of course you can."

Mandy dumped her bag on the floor and ran up the stairs, James close behind. She pushed open the spare bedroom door. On a little table near the radiator was the hamster's cage.

"We can't make any loud noises," Mandy whispered. "Hamsters are easily frightened." She peered into the cage. It was big and had a raised platform with a ladder leading up to it. There was a wheel for Frisky to exercise on, and a gnawing block so he could sharpen his teeth. Frisky was inside a wooden box on top of the platform. His little face was peeping out of a nest of soft hay.

Mandy drew in her breath. "Oh, look, James! Isn't he sweet?"

Frisky gazed out at her with jet black, shiny eyes. His nose twitched and his whiskers wiggled.

"He's gorgeous," James said in a hushed voice. "Will he come out, do you think?"

"We might have to wait until it starts to get dark," Mandy said. She knew hamsters usually slept in the daytime.

But as Mandy spoke, Frisky suddenly pushed his way through the hay and popped out onto his platform. He sat up on his hind legs and began washing his face. His paws had four fingers

each. His little body was round and plump and his fur was brownish-gray.

Mandy was delighted. She put her finger through the bars of the cage and wiggled it.

"He's very tiny." James peered closer.

"Dad told me he's a Russian hamster," Mandy said. "He said they're much smaller than the golden hamsters that most people have."

"What's that in the corner of the cage?" James pointed to a place where it looked as if Frisky had piled the sawdust up in a heap.

"That must be his food store," Mandy said.

"Food store?" James said, looking puzzled.

"Yes," said Mandy. "Hamsters always make a food store. In the wild they live in the desert so they never know where their next meal's coming from. With a food store they can eat whenever they like."

"I see," said James. "What a good idea."

"You seem to know a lot about it, Mandy." Grandpa's voice came from the doorway.

Mandy turned, her eyes shining. "Mom gave me one of those pamphlets they keep in the clinic. You know, the ones that tell you all about your pet and how to take care of it."

"Oh, yes." Grandpa bent to peer at Frisky. "What do you think of the little guy?"

"He's great," said Mandy and James together. They laughed.

"Can we take him out and play with him?" asked James.

"I think we'd better let him settle down first," Grandpa said. "Come and see him again tomorrow. I'm sure he'll be used to his vacation home by then."

There was a bag of hamster mix on the floor beside the table. The mix was made up of seeds and cereal flakes and dried fruit. There was also a bag of wood shavings for the bottom of Frisky's cage and a bundle of hay for his nest-box.

"Maybe he should have a few more toys," Mandy said to Grandpa and James when they were on their way down the stairs. "Hamsters get bored very easily."

"You're the expert," Grandpa said. He went to put the kettle on to make a cup of tea.

Grandma was still clattering away in her study.

"Tea, Dorothy!" Grandpa called. "Want some lemonade, you two?"

"Yes, please," they both said.

Mandy was looking thoughtful. "I'll bring Frisky a tube tomorrow," she said. "You know, one of those from the inside of a paper towel roll."

"What for?" asked James.

"For him to run in and out of," Mandy said. She sat down at the table. "Oh, Grandpa, I can't wait to play with him."

Grandma came in for her cup of tea.

"Frisky has been asleep since Mary brought him over," she said. "So I haven't had a good look at him yet."

"Well, he's awake now, Grandma," Mandy said. "And you can take it from me." Mandy's eyes shone. "He's just gorgeous!"

2

Grandma's Good Idea

When Grandma had finished her tea, Mandy and James took her to see Frisky. As they went into the spare bedroom, they heard a squeaking noise.

Frisky was wide awake and was inside his exercise wheel, running as fast as he could. The wheel was whizzing around so fast that it was almost a blur. Then Frisky dived out and ran up and down his ladder as fast as he could go.

James and Mandy burst out laughing.

Grandma was peering into the cage. "Well, I never," she said, looking amazed.

Frisky stopped dashing around his cage and sat on his hind legs to gnaw a sunflower seed.

"I'll bring him a bit of carrot tomorrow," Mandy said. "And a piece of apple."

"Apple *and* carrot?" Grandma laughed.

"Yes," Mandy said. "And celery and lettuce. Hamsters need things like that to keep them healthy."

Grandma was still peering at Frisky. "He looks a little like a mouse to me." She didn't sound sure whether she liked him or not.

"I suppose he does a little," Mandy said.

"But a nice mouse," James said.

Grandma gave a little shiver. "You might think mice are nice, James," she said. "But I don't think I do."

Mandy laughed. "Well, Frisky's adorable anyway, don't you think?"

Grandma still didn't look very sure. "I'll get used to him, I expect," she said.

"We could help you look after him if you like," Mandy said. "Couldn't we, James?"

"We certainly could," James said.

"That would be wonderful," said Grandma.

"And Grandpa says we can play with him when he's settled down," Mandy said. "We'll come tomorrow if that's okay?"

"Fine with me," Grandma said. "I've got a busy week ahead, so I'd be grateful if you'd keep Frisky busy."

"We will!" they both said at once.

They said good-bye to Grandma and Grandpa and made their way home. It was getting dark by now and a gray mist was settling over the village green.

"Bye, James," Mandy said as they parted at James's gate. "I'll come by for you in the morning."

Mandy felt happy as she ran off toward Animal Ark. Helping Grandma and Grandpa look after Frisky would be almost like having a hamster of her own.

A white van with TONY BROWN, PAINTER AND DECORATOR written in big letters on the side stood outside the gate of Animal Ark. The clinic and the house were getting a new coat of paint.

Mandy ran down the brick path and burst in through the door. "Mom! Mom! Where are you?"

"Here, Mandy," Dr. Emily Hope called from the examining room. Mandy ran through.

"Oh, Mom, you must go and see Frisky," she said excitedly. "He's so clever and cute! He's got an exercise wheel and he runs around like mad."

Dr. Emily was hunting for something in a box on the floor. Dr. Adam Hope was out on a call.

"I'll go over as soon as I can," Dr. Emily said. "I'm dying to meet him." She frowned. "Now where is that box of bandages? I can't find a thing since that decorator arrived."

Mandy moved aside another cardboard box

and perched herself up on the examining table. She'd had to pack up all her toys and books and take down her animal posters because her bedroom was going to be decorated, too. "I wish I could have a hamster of my own," she sighed.

"Sorry, Mandy." Dr. Emily was still looking through the box. "You know the rules. We just haven't got time to look after pets."

"Yes, I know." Mandy brightened up. "Never mind, playing with Frisky during my vacation will be almost as good."

Dr. Emily suddenly gave a shout. "Here it is! I knew it was here somewhere." She took out a box of bandages and put it on top of the cabinet. Then she gave Mandy a quick hug. "I'm sure Grandma will be grateful for your help. She's really busy this week organizing a rummage sale in the village hall."

"Maybe James and I could help her with that, too?" Mandy said.

"I'm sure you could," Dr. Emily said. "It looks as if you're going to have lots to do this vacation."

"Yep," Mandy said. "Then there's the fireworks display. James and I promised to help build the bonfire." She frowned. "I hope people will remember to keep their pets in. They get really scared of fireworks."

There was going to be a huge bonfire and fireworks display in the field behind the village green. Everyone in the village would be going. James's dad was on the organizing committee.

"I'll get Jean to put a reminder on the board in the waiting room," Dr. Emily said. Jean Knox was Animal Ark's receptionist.

"That's a great idea, Mom," Mandy said.

She got down off the examining table and went out to the back room. There were several animals out there. In one wire cage, a large white rabbit with pink eyes was nibbling a carrot.

"What's this bunny here for, Mom?" Mandy called. She opened the cage door and gently stroked the rabbit's fur.

Dr. Emily came into the room. "He's had a infected foot," she explained. "It's much better now so he's going home tomorrow."

A small black cat was asleep in another cage. Mandy went to look. "What about him?" she asked.

"He's a she," Dr. Emily said with a smile. "She's having an operation tomorrow."

"Poor thing." Mandy gazed at the sleeping cat. She always felt very sad at the thought of animals being sick.

"She's not sick," Dr. Emily explained. "She's just having an operation to prevent her from having kittens."

One of the cages was covered with a dark cloth. Mandy lifted a corner and peeped in. A creature about the size of a small rabbit was curled up in a ball in one corner. Mandy drew in her breath.

"What's *that*?"

"A chinchilla," Dr. Emily said.

The chinchilla stirred and stretched. Mandy could see it had thick silver-gray fur, long ears, and a bushy tail.

"He is beautiful!" Mandy said. She thought the chinchilla was one of the prettiest animals she had ever seen.

"Yes," Dr. Emily said. "They're quite unusual."

"When did he come in, Mom?" asked Mandy.

"Yesterday," Dr. Emily said. "I'm afraid he's not well."

"Oh, no. What's wrong with him?"

"Some kind of lung infection, we think. He's had some medicine and seems to be getting a little better."

"I'd love to cuddle him." Mandy looked longingly at the little gray creature.

"Maybe when he's better." Dr. Emily glanced at the clock on the wall. "Come on, Mandy. Dad will be back soon."

Mandy took one last look at the animals and followed Dr. Emily into the house.

It wasn't long before Dr. Adam walked in. Mandy told him all about Frisky before he had even had time to take his coat off. He laughed when she told him about the exercise wheel.

"Does it squeak?" he asked.

Mandy grinned. "Yes, it does a little."

"Put a little cooking oil on it," Dr. Adam said. "That will fix it and it won't do the hamster any harm if he happens to lick it."

"I'll tell Grandma," Mandy said.

They had just finished dinner when the phone rang.

"I'll answer it." Mandy ran through the hall.

"Mandy!" It was Grandma and she sounded worried.

"What's up?" Mandy asked.

"It's Frisky," Grandma said. "There's something wrong with him. Can you get Mom or Dad to come and take a look at him?"

"Oh, yes, of course," Mandy said. "We'll come right away." Her stomach turned over. She didn't think she could bear it if Frisky was sick.

She dashed back into the kitchen.

"Mom, Dad," she gasped. "Can you come with me to Grandma's? There's something wrong with Frisky."

"Oh, dear." Dr. Emily took off her apron. "I'll go. Dad can stay here in case there are any emergency calls. Is that all right, Adam?"

Dr. Adam was sitting at the table reading his vet's magazine. "Yes, go ahead. I hope Frisky's all right."

"Oh, so do I," Mandy said.

"We'll take the car," Dr. Emily said when they got outside. "Just in case Frisky needs to come back to the clinic."

Mandy felt very worried as she climbed into the car next to her mom. Frisky had been all right when she and James were at Lilac Cottage earlier.

They found Grandma waiting for them when they arrived. She hurried up the stairs in front of them and thrust open the door to Frisky's room.

"I think he's got mumps," she said anxiously.

Dr. Emily took one look at Frisky and burst out laughing.

"It's not funny, Emily!" Grandma sounded indignant. "Look at him!"

Frisky was sitting on top of his nest-box. He gazed at them with beady, bright eyes. His face was huge. His cheeks were puffed out to three times their normal size.

"Oh, Mom!" Dr. Emily laughed and shook her head. "He hasn't got mumps; he's storing food in his cheek pouches!"

"What?" Grandma was peering at Frisky with a worried look on her face.

Dr. Emily quickly told Grandma that hamsters have large pouches in their cheeks in which to keep food. She pointed to his store

in the corner. "They have a food store, too. Look."

Grandma began to laugh, too. "Oh, dear," she said, wiping her eyes. "What a silly woman I am." She turned to Mandy. "Honestly, Mandy, I know absolutely nothing about hamsters."

"Never mind, Grandma," Mandy said.

"Look," Grandma said, "I've got an idea. Why don't you come and stay here for your vacation, Mandy? You could be full-time resident hamster-keeper for me." She turned to

Mandy's mom. "What do you think, Emily?"

"I think it would be a nice idea," Dr. Emily said. "It's not much fun at Animal Ark at the moment with ladders and cans of paint all over the place. How about it, Mandy?"

Mandy's eyes were shining. Stay with Grandma and look after Frisky for a whole week? It would be fantastic. "Oh, Mom," she said. "Can I really?"

Dr. Emily gave her a hug. "Really," she said. "It will save you from running over here every five minutes."

"Hear that, Frisky?" said Mandy. "I'm going to stay here and look after you."

Frisky gazed at her and twitched his nose.

Mandy looked up at her grandma. "He says it's a good idea."

Grandma chuckled. "I can see he's going to have the vacation of a lifetime."

"Yes," Mandy said. "And so am I."

3

A Spring Cleaning

In the morning Mandy jumped out of bed, dressed quickly, and packed a few clothes in her bag. She ran downstairs, ducking under a ladder in the hallway.

Tony Brown was at the top of the ladder painting the ceiling. There were a couple of large paint cans lying open on the floor.

"Morning, Mandy," Tony called as Mandy sidled past. "Off from school?"

"Yes, I am," Mandy said. She told him where she was going.

"Hamster, eh?" Tony came down the ladder. "Nice things, hamsters. I had one when I was a kid. His name was Lazy."

"Lazy!" Mandy exclaimed. "That's a funny name."

"It wasn't for him," Tony said with a grin. "He slept most of the time."

Mandy laughed. She hoped Frisky wouldn't sleep *all* the time, otherwise she would never get to play with him.

In the kitchen, Dr. Emily and Dr. Adam were sitting at the breakfast table.

Dr. Adam looked up from his morning paper. "Off to Hamster Hotel, Mandy?" he said.

"Hamster Hotel!" Mandy laughed. "That's a great name!"

"Frisky's a very lucky little fellow." Dr. Emily got up and put on her white vet's coat. It was almost time for morning clinic hours. "He'll be the best looked–after hamster in Welford."

"I hope so," Mandy said as she opened a drawer.

"What are you looking for, Mandy?" her mom asked.

Mandy quickly explained. "Hamsters love running in and out of tunnels," she said. I'm looking for the middle of a paper towel roll.

"There's one in the clinic, I think. Come through with me." Mandy followed her mom. "You mustn't give him anything made of soft plastic to play with, you know, Mandy," Dr. Emily said.

"I won't," Mandy said quickly. "He's got very sharp teeth. He'd only bite through it."

"That's right. Plastic wouldn't do his tummy any good at all."

Jean Knox was at her desk opening the day's mail.

"Hello, Jean," Mandy said. "I'm going to be staying at Hamster Hotel for my vacation." She grinned.

"Hamster Hotel?" Jean looked at Mandy over the top of her glasses. "Where on earth's that?"

Mandy told her.

Jean laughed. "Have fun."

After breakfast, Mandy washed up, then picked up her bag. "Well, Dad," she said. "I'm leaving now."

Dr. Adam kissed her good-bye. "Me, too," he said. "I've got to go up to Skye Farm to look at a sick calf. Have a great time, Mandy." He went into the clinic to get his bag.

On the way to Lilac Cottage, Mandy met Walter Pickard walking to the general store. Walter was an old friend of Mandy's grandpa. They were both bell-ringers at the village church.

"Where are you going, young lady?" Walter asked when he saw Mandy walking along with her bag. He laughed when she told him she was going to Hamster Hotel.

"And I'd better hurry," she said. "It's time for Frisky's breakfast. Oh, you won't forget to keep your cats in on Thursday evening, will you, Mr. Pickard?"

Mandy was very fond of Walter's three lively cats, Missie, Tom, and Scraps.

Walter frowned. "Thursday evening?"

"Yes," Mandy reminded him. "Bonfire night. There will be lots and lots of fireworks."

"Oh, yes, of course," Walter said. "Thanks for reminding me."

Before she went on to Lilac Cottage, Mandy went to James's to tell him the good news.

"Lucky you. All those yummy cakes," James said. He loved Grandma's baking.

Mandy laughed. "Why don't you come over when you've had breakfast?" she said. "We'll clean Frisky's cage out and play with him if he's awake."

"Great." James was trying to stop Blackie from running out the door. "See you later."

At Lilac Cottage, Grandma had just finished typing out a notice announcing the rummage sale.

"Ah, Mandy," she said as Mandy came in and dumped her bag on the chair. "Just the person I wanted to see."

"How's Frisky this morning?" Mandy asked.

"I peeped into his room, but he must have been asleep."

Mandy felt disappointed. She would have loved to say hello to Frisky, but she knew it would be wrong to disturb him. It looked as if she would have to be up very early in the morning to catch him before he dozed off.

"I'm not surprised he was asleep," Grandma said. "I could hear him whizzing around on that wheel all night. He's probably tired out."

Mandy told her about Dr. Adam's suggestion to stop the wheel from squeaking.

"We can oil it when we clean the cage out," she said.

"Well," Grandma said. "After you've done that, will you do something for *me*?"

"Of course I will, Grandma." Mandy took her bag into the hall. She would unpack her things later.

Grandma was still gazing at the ad she had typed out:

SUPER RUMMAGE SALE
VILLAGE HALL, 2 PM SATURDAY
TO BENEFIT THE CHURCH
OF WELFORD
Please take any sale items to
Lilac Cottage before Friday.

"Do you think this is all right, Mandy?" she asked.

"Looks fine to me." Mandy looked over Grandma's shoulder.

"Good." Grandma rolled up the ad. "Do you think Jean would make some photocopies for me?"

"I'm sure she would," Mandy said.

"And do you think you and James could hang them around the village?" Grandma asked. "I want as many people to know about the sale as possible."

"Okay, Grandma," Mandy said. "No problem."

"The priest might put one on the church bulletin board," Grandma said thoughtfully.

"Right." Mandy fiddled with her fingers. She was getting impatient to see Frisky. "And I'll ask Jean to put one up at Animal Ark," she said.

"Great," Grandma said. "I'm afraid it's short notice. I've been so busy I haven't had time to advertise until now." She got up. "Never mind, people usually come to a rummage sale."

Mandy was hovering anxiously near the door. "Can I clean Frisky's cage out before I go?"

Grandma smiled and gave her a hug. "Of course," she said. "Pets come first!"

Mandy was halfway up the stairs when there was a knock at the door. She ran back down.

James stood on the doorstep. "I came as quickly as I could," he said. He held up a bag with a carrot and an apple inside. "I've brought Frisky's breakfast."

"Great! Thanks, James. Come on in," she said. "We've got a million things to do today."

At first, Frisky was nowhere to be seen. But when Mandy bent down to peep into his nest she could just see a hint of gray-brown fur among the soft hay of his bed. There he was, curled up tight as a ball, and fast asleep.

"Is it okay to clean the cage out now?" James asked.

"If we're very careful." Mandy gently un-latched the door of Frisky's cage. "And we shouldn't disturb his food store," she said.

Mandy carefully took out all the old pieces of food and wood shavings from the bottom. She put them on some newspaper and wrapped them up. Then she spread out some clean shavings. She put Frisky's toys back in, together with the cardboard roll she had brought from Animal Ark.

Meanwhile, James took Frisky's water bottle and filled it with clean water from the bathroom sink. Frisky's little china food bowl needed filling up, too. James poured some hamster mix into it, then added a piece of apple and carrot.

"A feast," he said.

Mandy smiled. "Hamster Hotel is famous for its good food," she laughed.

Finally, Mandy dabbed a drop of cooking oil on the center of Frisky's wheel. She spun it around. There wasn't a squeak to be heard.

"There we are," she said when she had finished. "All cleaned."

Frisky had slept through the whole thing. Mandy peered into the nest hopefully. Maybe

he would wake up, just for five minutes? But there was no sign of movement. Mandy sighed. They really would have to wait until later to play with him.

"Come on," she whispered to James. She picked up the bundle of newspapers. "Let's come back after lunch. I want to put some of Grandma's posters up around the village."

"Okay," James said in a hushed voice.

They tiptoed out of the room and went downstairs.

"What should I do with this, Grandma?" Mandy asked.

Grandma looked at the bundle of newspapers. "You can put it outside," she said.

"I'll do it." James took the papers from Mandy and went outside. Mandy went down the path with Grandma's rummage sale poster. Soon James caught up to her, and together they made their way toward Animal Ark.

The priest of the Welford church, Reverend Hadcroft, was sitting in the waiting room with a cat basket at his feet. Jean was on the phone.

"Hello, Mr. Hadcroft," Mandy and James said as they came through the door.

"Hello, you two," Mr. Hadcroft said.

Mandy sat down beside him. She peered into the basket. "What's wrong with Jemima? I hope she's not sick."

"No, she's due for a shot, that's all."

Mandy felt relieved. She loved the priest's tabby cat and would have hated for her to be sick.

Dr. Emily's head appeared around the clinic door. "Mr. Hadcroft?" she called.

Mr. Hadcroft picked up Jemima's basket. "See you later, Mandy. See you later, James."

Jean Knox was still on the phone. She was talking to Mrs. Ponsonby about her Pekinese, Pandora.

"Yes, yes," she was saying. "Dr. Adam will come as soon as he can."

"Is Pandora ill?" Mandy asked anxiously when Jean put the phone down.

Jean shook her head. "No, just short of breath," she said. "She needs to go on a diet. That woman spoils her dog rotten."

Mandy showed Jean Grandma's posters. "Do you mind if I make some copies?"

"Help yourself," Jean said.

"Thanks," said Mandy as she and James went to the back room where the photocopier was kept.

"A dozen should be enough," Mandy said. When they'd finished, she took one out to Jean. "Could you put this up on the board, please, Jean?"

"Will do," Jean said. "Now shoo, you two, I'm very busy."

Mandy and James ran out and made their way down to the general store. Then they worked their way around the village shops. Soon there were posters everywhere.

Mandy hoped Grandma's rummage sale would be a great success!

4

Missing!

When Mandy and James got back to Lilac Cottage, Grandma was busy sorting out things for the rummage sale. She had filled two black plastic bags full of old clothes and books. Mandy helped her carry them upstairs.

"About time we got rid of some of this

junk," Grandma muttered. "Your grandpa *will* insist on hoarding things, Mandy."

Mandy giggled. Grandpa *never* threw anything away if he could help it.

"I'm afraid they'll have to go in your room for now, Mandy. There's not really anywhere else to put them." Grandma dumped the bags by the closet door. "Someone will come by on Friday to pick them up."

Mandy peered hopefully into Frisky's cage. But he was still asleep. The cage was very neat. Mandy tried not to be disappointed. She would just have to be patient. There would be plenty of time to play with Frisky that evening.

And when she and James went upstairs after dinner, there was Frisky, sitting at the bottom of his ladder, nibbling on a piece of apple.

Mandy drew in her breath. "Isn't he wonderful?" She put her finger through the bars and wiggled it. Frisky finished his apple and ran over to his food bowl. Soon he was gobbling up his hamster mix. Most of it went into his cheek pouches.

"He looks as if he's got mumps again," James laughed. He had heard all about Grandma's mistake. "Why don't we take him down to show your grandma and grandpa?"

Grandma was getting ready to go out. There was a meeting of the rummage sale committee and Grandma was chairman.

She peered into the cage. "Oh, yes." She still didn't sound too sure. "He is very sweet."

Mandy put the cage on the coffee table in the living room where Grandpa was watching his favorite gardening program.

Frisky had finished his meal and was running in and out of the cardboard tube.

Grandpa looked into the cage. "What a cute little fellow," he said. "Should we let him out to have a run around the room?"

Mandy's eyes lit up. It was just what she and James had been waiting for.

"Oh, Grandpa, can we?" she said.

Grandpa cocked his head to one side. "I think we'd better wait until your grandma's gone, though, don't you? She might not like him running around the living room."

Grandma poked her head in the door. "I'm leaving now, Tom," she said.

"Okay." Grandpa waved his hand. "See you later."

They waited until they heard the door bang shut.

"Okay," Grandpa said. "Coast's clear. Let's make sure there are no holes for him to disappear down, first."

James and Mandy searched the room thoroughly.

"No holes!" they said.

"And all the windows are shut," Mandy added.

"I'll put the guard around the fireplace." Grandpa got up and put the big brass screen in front of the fire. "There, that should be okay."

Mandy was so excited, her heart was beating like a drum as she opened the cage door. She put her hand slowly inside. She picked the hamster up gently and lifted him out.

Frisky sat on the palm of her hand looking at her. "I think he likes me," Mandy said.

"Smart little one," Grandpa chuckled.

Suddenly Frisky turned and ran up Mandy's arm. He sat on her shoulder, then disappeared inside the collar of her sweatshirt. She sat perfectly still. She could feel Frisky running down her back and around her waist. It tickled so much, it was all she could do to stop herself from wiggling. Then, suddenly, he appeared on her lap.

"Could I hold him?" James had been watching.

"Of course you can."

Mandy picked Frisky up and passed him to James. He stroked the hamster and then put him on his knee. Frisky suddenly ran around James's waist and disappeared.

James sat as still as a stone. "Where did he go?" He hardly dared breathe.

"I don't know," Mandy said.

Then a lump appeared in the pocket of James's sweatshirt.

Grandpa roared with laughter. "He's in your pocket," he said. "The clever little fellow."

Suddenly Frisky's nose appeared and he scampered out of James's pocket, down the side of the chair, and onto the floor. He ran around, then disappeared under the sideboard.

Mandy lay flat on the floor. She could see Frisky sitting on his hind legs. He was gazing back at her with bright, beady eyes.

Suddenly, the door opened and Grandma came in.

"I forgot my notebook," she said, heading for her study.

"Grandma!" Mandy gasped. "Shut the . . ."

But it was too late; Frisky had spotted the opening. He dropped down on all fours and scurried out of the room as fast as he could.

"Oh, no," Mandy wailed. "He's escaped!" She dashed into the hall.

Grandma looked around. "Who has?"

"Frisky," James said. He ran out after Mandy.

Grandpa sat in his chair, chuckling. "He won't go far, Mandy," he called. "Don't worry." Then he suddenly looked serious. "I hope you shut the back door, Dorothy."

"Yes, I did," she said.

"Thank goodness for that," Grandpa said.

By now Frisky had completely disappeared. Mandy and James ran all over looking for him.

"Do you think he could have gotten up the stairs?" James asked.

Mandy shook her head. She felt close to tears. "I don't know," she wailed.

Grandma came back out with her notebook. She was walking very carefully, afraid she might step on the runaway hamster.

"You'll have to find him, Mandy." Grandma looked serious. "Mary won't be very pleased if she comes back from vacation and he's missing."

"I know, Grandma, I'm really sorry," Mandy said, close to tears.

Grandma put her arms around her. "It was my fault for opening that door."

Mandy shook her head. "No, it wasn't. I shouldn't have let him out. I just wanted to hold him." A tear ran down her cheek.

Grandma gave her a quick hug. "Don't worry, Mandy, he's got to be in the house somewhere. If he's still missing, I'll help look when I get back." She slipped out the back door, shutting it quickly behind her.

Mandy and James searched for Frisky until it was time for James to go home.

Mandy's face was sad as she said good-bye to him at the front door.

"I just don't know what we're going to do," she said. She couldn't bear to think of the little creature lost somewhere.

"You could make a trap," James suggested.

Mandy looked at him in horror. "What? Like a mousetrap?"

"No, silly," James said. "A bottle."

Mandy looked puzzled. "What do you mean?"

"Well," James said. "You get a tall glass jar, and put some food and bedding in it."

"Then what?" Mandy asked.

"Then you leave it sideways on the floor. When the hamster goes in to get the food, he won't be able to climb out through the neck because it's too slippery."

Mandy's face brightened. "How do you know all this?"

"I read it in a book," James said. He zipped up his coat. "It's supposed to work every time."

"James, you're so smart!" Mandy cried.

"I know." James laughed as he let himself out through the front door.

Mandy closed the door behind him and sighed. She hoped James was right about the hamster trap. If not, she didn't know *what* they were going to do.

"Any sign of the little fellow?" Grandpa asked when Mandy got back into the front room.

She shook her head. "No." She went on to tell Grandpa about James's idea.

"Sounds good." Grandpa turned off the television.

"One of those tall jars Grandma uses for bottling fruit would be ideal. There's a whole shelf of them in the pantry." While Grandpa got one down, Mandy went upstairs and got some hamster mix and bedding. She took a piece of carrot and a piece of apple. If they didn't tempt Frisky, then nothing would.

"We'll put it in the living room," Grandpa said. "Let's hope he finds it."

That night Mandy lay awake. She kept imagining all sorts of things that might have happened to Frisky. What if he were stuck somewhere? Maybe he was hiding in a closet? She had looked for him again before she went to bed, but there was no trace of the hamster anywhere.

In the middle of the night Mandy awoke from a restless sleep. The moon was shining brightly through the gap in her curtains. Mandy got out of bed and crept downstairs. It was no good trying to sleep. She *had* to see if Frisky was in the jar.

Mandy tiptoed into the living room. Grandma had drawn back the curtains and the room was bright with moonlight. The jar lay just where Mandy had left it. She let out a sigh of disappointment.

The jar was empty!

5

Never a Dull Moment

Mandy felt close to tears. Then she suddenly realized the apple and the carrot were gone from the jar. The little bundle of hay began to twitch, and all of a sudden out popped Frisky. He ran toward the neck of the jar but kept slipping and sliding backward. James had been right. Frisky couldn't escape.

"Frisky!" Mandy almost shouted for joy. "Thank goodness!" She scooped up the jar and carried it up to her bedroom. "You naughty boy," she scolded as she climbed the stairs. "Don't you ever frighten me like that again!"

As she went along the landing, Grandma's bedroom door opened. Grandma appeared, looking sleepy-eyed.

"Are you all right, Mandy? I heard you go downstairs."

"Yes, thanks, Grandma. I'm fine." She held up the jar. "Look!"

"Well, thank goodness for that," Grandma said with a sigh. "Is he all right?"

"He's fine," Mandy said.

"Now perhaps we can get some sleep," Grandma said. "Grandpa's been tossing and turning ever since we got to bed. Who would have thought such a little creature would cause so much worry?" She wagged her finger at Frisky. "Now you behave yourself, young fellow!" She winked at Mandy, then went back into her room and closed the door.

Mandy took Frisky into her room. She gently shook him out of the jar and popped him back into his cage. Frisky ran to his exercise wheel, hopped in, and began running. The wheel whizzed around and around. He wasn't affected at all from his adventure.

Mandy climbed back into bed and was asleep almost as soon as her head touched the pillow.

The next morning she called James to tell him the good news.

"Can I bring Blackie over?" James said after she told him the story. "We said we'd do some training with him, remember?"

"Okay," Mandy said. She smiled to herself. Training Blackie was always fun, although not really successful!

Grandpa was just going out to do some work in the garden. He was in a strange mood that morning. Mandy had heard him opening and closing drawers and muttering to himself. Then he had stomped downstairs, grabbed a coat from the hall closet, and gone out, still mumbling something under his breath.

"Could you take that barrel of cuttings to the bonfire later, please, Mandy?" he asked as she stepped outside to see if James and Blackie were coming. "They're dry and should burn very well."

Just then James and Blackie appeared at the side of the cottage. Blackie had his ball in his mouth. He barged through the gate, almost pulling James over.

"Dad's got some old wood for the bonfire," James panted. "I promised him we'd bring that over, too. But maybe we'll do some training with Blackie first?"

"Sure," Mandy said.

Grandpa grinned. He had seen them trying to train Blackie before. "Good luck," he said and disappeared into his garden shed.

Grandma was just going off to her exercise class. Mandy went with her to the front gate.

"If anyone brings any goods for the sale, don't forget it's got to go upstairs," Grandma reminded her. "I don't want it cluttering up the hall and front room."

"I won't," Mandy promised. "See you later, Grandma." She waved as Grandma headed off in the direction of the village hall. Then she turned to James. "What are we going to do with Blackie today?" she asked.

"Retrieving," James said. He tried to get the ball out of Blackie's mouth. Blackie growled playfully and twisted his head from side to side. "Labradors are good at that."

"Stay!" Mandy shook her finger at Blackie.

Blackie stared at her from under his eyelids.

"Stay!" she said again.

"Here, Blackie." James took a dog biscuit from his pocket. Blackie dropped the ball and gobbled up the biscuit. Mandy dived for the ball.

"Okay," she said. "Here we go."

Mandy and James spent the whole morning trying to get Blackie to bring the ball back. No matter how hard they tried, Blackie would insist on running off around the garden with it.

Grandpa thought it was better than a comedy show. "You'll have to put him on a long leash and *make* him bring it back," he called, laughing. He leaned on his spade, watching Blackie running around with Mandy and James chasing him.

"It's no good," James panted. "I give up. Blackie's no good at bringing things back and that's that."

Just then a fancy car pulled up outside. A large lady got out. She was wearing a tweed suit and a black hat. It was Mrs. Ponsonby. Pandora the Pekinese was peeping out of the window from her special compartment at the back.

"Dr. Adam!" Mrs. Ponsonby was at the back of the car in three long strides. "I've brought some things for the sale."

"Oh, good morning, Mrs. Ponsonby," Grandpa called. He put down his spade and hurried to the gate. "That's very kind of you, thank you very much."

"There's one of darling Pandora's old baskets." Mrs. Ponsonby opened the trunk. "And some other things." She piled the basket and several cardboard boxes into Grandpa's arms.

James and Mandy ran to help when they saw Grandpa was having a problem balancing all the boxes in his arms. Mandy said hello to Pandora as she passed, then ran to take a box.

Blackie, meanwhile, lay on the grass, the ball clamped firmly between his jaws.

"How's Pandora, Mrs. Ponsonby?" Mandy asked.

"She's hasn't been well," Mrs. Ponsonby replied. "But I've kept her in bed for a couple

of days and she seems a bit better. Aren't you, darling?" she cooed to Pandora.

Mandy peered through the window. "Maybe a long walk would do her good?" she suggested. "Most dogs love walks."

Mrs. Ponsonby shook her head. "It would only tire her out, poor lamb," she said.

Pandora was looking at Mandy with her black boot-button eyes. She gave a yap, then yawned. She lay down, sighed, and closed her eyes. Mandy smiled. Pandora obviously didn't think much of *that* idea. "Don't forget to keep her in on Thursday evening," she said.

"Thursday evening?" Mrs. Ponsonby looked puzzled.

"The bonfire," Mandy said.

"Oh, yes, of course!" Mrs. Ponsonby exclaimed. "Those horrible fireworks. Don't worry, I'll make sure Pandora is tucked safely in bed."

Mandy smiled again. Pandora certainly was the most spoiled dog around.

She helped Grandpa take the stuff upstairs.

"Someone else is here with some things," James called as they went back out into the garden.

"Phew." Grandpa took off his cap and wiped his brow. "*When* am I going to get my gardening done?"

By the time Thursday came, there was a great pile of stuff in Mandy's room. In fact there was so much, it had spilled out onto the landing. Boxes of books, old toys, clothes, all kinds of things.

"Grandma will be pleased," Mandy said as she helped Grandpa carry another load up the stairs.

"She certainly will," Grandpa said. "Everyone's gone crazy. Some of this stuff is as good as new."

Mandy smiled to herself. She thought of Grandpa's favorite old gardening sweater. He always said *that* was as good as new even though it was full of holes. Grandma was always telling him he should throw it away.

Every day Mandy and James made sure Frisky's cage was clean and that he had plenty of fresh food and water.

Frisky usually woke up in the afternoon. His antics kept Mandy and James laughing. There was certainly never a dull moment when Frisky was awake. And they were very careful never to let him escape again.

By now, the bonfire in the field behind the village green looked like a mountain. When they weren't looking after Frisky or taking Blackie for walks, Mandy and James helped to build it.

"I hope they're going to make sure no hedgehogs have crawled under it," Mandy said to James as they tipped yet another barrel of Grandpa's garden cuttings onto the heap.

"Dad built a platform first," James assured her. "That means they should be able to see if there are any underneath before they light it."

"Excellent," Mandy said. She grabbed the

empty barrel and ran on ahead. "I can't wait for tonight."

The bonfire was going to be lit at six o'clock. Mandy made sure Frisky had enough food and water for the evening, then put on her coat and boots.

Outside it was a chilly, misty evening. People were already making their way along the main street toward the field where the bonfire stood.

Mandy walked between Grandma and Grandpa. Her mom and dad were waiting for them outside Animal Ark. They were meeting James and Mrs. Hunter at the bonfire. Mr. Hunter had gone ahead earlier to make sure that the fireworks display was ready.

"While I think of it, Mandy," her mom said as they strolled past the general store and down the narrow alley that led to the bonfire field. "Would you like to come shopping in Walton tomorrow?"

"That would be great," Mandy said. "I bet James would like to come, too. I'll ask him."

Her eyes lit up as she suddenly had an idea. "I could get Frisky a present to remind him of his vacation at Hamster Hotel!"

Dr. Emily smiled. "How's he doing?"

"He's fine," Mandy said. She tried not to think about how much she would miss Frisky when Mary came to get him.

A large crowd had gathered around the bonfire. Almost everyone in the village had turned up.

Mandy ran off to find James. He was standing behind the ropes, watching his dad getting ready to light the huge bonfire.

There was a stall nearby selling hot dogs and hot baked potatoes, and the smell made Mandy's stomach rumble.

She asked James if he would like to go shopping the following day. "I'm going to get Frisky a present," she told him.

"That sounds great!" James jumped up and down to try to keep warm. "Maybe we could buy a really good one from both of us?"

"Let's go and see your dad." Mandy scrambled under the rope and ran over to Mr. Hunter. James followed.

"Have you checked for hedgehogs?" Mandy asked anxiously.

Mr. Hunter confirmed that he had. "There weren't any," he said. "Now get back behind the ropes, please, you two," he added. "It's not safe here."

When Mandy and James rejoined the crowd, Mr. Hunter lit the fuse, and there was a shout as the bonfire caught and roared. The orange flames lit up the night sky. Everyone clapped.

Then, with a bang and a shower of sparks, the fireworks display began.

Even though she was enjoying herself, Mandy couldn't help worrying about the village pets.

"I hope everyone remembered to keep their dogs and cats in," she said in James's ear after a very loud bang that echoed around the field like thunder.

"Well, Blackie and Benji are inside my house safe and sound," James said.

Mandy suddenly decided she couldn't resist the smell of the hot dogs any longer.

"Do you want a hot dog, James?"

"Mmm." James licked his lips. "Yes, please."

They wandered over to the stall where Mr. Oliver was dishing out the food.

Mandy had just finished eating when she spotted a dark shadow by the hedge. She clutched James's arm.

"James, look! What's that over there?"

James peered into the shadows. "Where?"

Mandy pointed. She couldn't believe her eyes. A small black dog was creeping along the edge of the field.

"There!" she cried. "Come on, James, quick!" Mandy ran across, James right behind her.

By now, the little creature was crouched by the gate, hunched up, its tail between its legs. It was trembling with fright. It flinched as a rocket took off and exploded in a blizzard of stars.

Just as it was about to dash off into the road, Mandy grabbed it. The dog was freezing cold and whimpering with fear. Mandy crouched down and scooped him up into her arms. She noticed he was wearing a collar with a silver tag attached to it.

"Oh, James, he's terrified." She stroked the dog's head. How could anyone be so cruel as to let their dog out on a night like this?

"Poor thing," Mandy was murmuring.

"Come on, James, let's get him away from the noise."

Cradling the dog against her coat, Mandy walked through the gate.

"Where are you taking him?" James hurried after her.

"Back to Animal Ark," she said. "He'll be safe there."

Grandma and Grandpa were talking to Walter Pickard. Mandy waited while James ran to tell them where they were going. Then they headed off across the village green toward Animal Ark. The dog was trembling and making little whining noises.

"Don't worry," Mandy soothed. "You're safe now." She unzipped her jacket and put it around him. The sooner they got the little dog into the warmth of Animal Ark, the better.

6

A Present for Frisky

Mandy got a blanket and wrapped it around the little dog. She sat by the fire, hugging him on her lap. James bent to stroke his head. The dog had stopped shaking and had nestled as close to Mandy as he could.

"Here," Mandy said to James. "You hold him

while I heat up some milk. It'll warm his
tummy up and make him feel much better."

A few minutes later Mandy poured the milk
carefully into a small bowl. James put the dog
down on the floor. He wobbled a bit, then
sniffed the milk. Soon he began to lap it up.
Mandy kneeled beside him.

"I wonder why his owners didn't shut him
in," she said. "They should have known how
scared he'd be."

"Look at his collar," James said. "It should
tell us where he lives."

Mandy turned over the silver tag. "His name's Bobby," she said. "And there's just a phone number. Welford 876597." She stood up. "I'd better call them. They'll probably be worried about him."

Just then the door opened and Dr. Adam came hurrying in. He had come as soon as he heard what had happened. "Grandma told me you were here." He bent down. "Is he all right?"

The little dog had finished the milk. He sat huddled up close to the fire. He was licking his lips and looking at Dr. Adam with wide, scared eyes.

Dr. Adam held his head and looked into his eyes. He ran his hand down his back and legs. "He seems okay now."

Mandy gave the little puppy a hug. "His name's Bobby," Mandy said. "I was just going to call his owners."

She went out into the hall to use the phone. A minute or two later, she came back. "He comes from those houses behind the church," she said. "I said we'd take him home."

"Did they know he was out?" James asked.

"Yes. They were really worried. He belongs to their little girl and she's been crying all evening. They said they had been looking everywhere for him. He's always running away."

"Well, this might have taught him a lesson," Dr. Adam said. "Although it's really up to the owners to keep their dogs under control."

Dr. Adam went to get a spare dog leash he kept in the clinic. When he came back, Mandy and James were ready to go.

"Grandma and Grandpa have gone home," Dr. Adam told her. "I'll give them a call to tell them you're on your way back."

"Thanks," Mandy said.

"We missed the rest of the fireworks," James said as they hurried along the main street toward the church.

"Oh, well," Mandy said. "I would rather have been helping Bobby anyway."

"Me, too," James agreed.

They found Bobby's house and knocked on the door. A little girl answered it. Her eyes were red and she looked very unhappy. Her face lit up though when she saw Mandy and James standing on the doorstep with Bobby.

When he saw her, Bobby's tail began wagging really fast. He gave a little whine and began jumping up at her.

The little girl burst into tears and bent down to pick him up.

"Oh, Bobby, you naughty boy!" she sobbed, burying her face in the soft fur of his neck.

Bobby began whining and licking her face.

"Oh, Bobby," she said again.

Mandy felt like crying, too. Bobby's owner had obviously been frantic.

"My dad says he's all right," Mandy said. "But he's had a very lucky escape," she added gently. "You'll have to keep a close eye on him from now on."

"We will, I promise." The girl wiped her eyes. "Thank you very much."

They could hear her still talking to Bobby as she turned back into the house and closed the door.

When Mandy had said good-bye to James and gotten back to Lilac Cottage, Grandma had a steaming cup of hot chocolate ready for her.

"How is the poor little dog?" she asked as Mandy came in.

"Okay," Mandy said. She told her grandma about the little girl.

"I bet you scolded her," Grandpa said when he came in. He knew how angry Mandy got if she thought animals were not being looked after properly.

"No, I didn't," Mandy said. "She was too upset."

Grandpa gave Mandy a hug. "Bobby was a very lucky dog if you ask me," he said.

Mandy finished her drink and ran upstairs to see Frisky. He was running around and around the cage, up his ladder, through his cardboard tunnel, and in and out of his exercise wheel.

The wheel was squeaking badly again. Cooking oil didn't seem to last very long.

Mandy decided that Frisky was the most adorable pet she had ever *almost* had, even though she sometimes got tired just watching him!

She sat by his cage and told Frisky about the night's adventures. He seemed to listen to every word she was saying. Then she took him out and let him have a little run around. She picked him up and he sat on her hand. Then he darted up her sleeve, sat on her collar for a moment, and disappeared down her neck.

Mandy chuckled. She was used to the feeling of Frisky running about inside her clothes by now. When he popped out of her sleeve again, she caught him and put him carefully back into his cage.

She sighed. She was really going to miss Frisky when it was time for him to go home.

The following morning Dr. Emily picked up Mandy and James to take them shopping. Before they left, Mandy went to see Frisky. He was very sleepy and almost ready for his day-time snooze.

"He's really sweet," Dr. Emily said. "And very clean and healthy. You're doing a great job, you two."

On the way to Walton, Mandy gazed out the window at the passing fields and trees. The mist of the early morning had given way to bright sunshine. Tomorrow she would be busy helping with the rummage sale, and the next day Frisky would be going home and she would be going back to Animal Ark. The week went by so quickly.

"What are we going to get Frisky?" James asked.

Mandy was thoughtful. "I'm not sure. We'll have to look and see what they've got in the pet shop."

"He's already got a wheel, a tube, and a gnawing block," James said.

Dr. Emily laughed. "Well, what *do* you buy the hamster who's got everything?"

"A friend?" James suggested.

Mandy shook her head. "No, hamsters have to live on their own. They fight if you put two together."

Dr. Emily came up with an idea. "You could make him an adventure playground," she suggested.

"Adventure playground?" Mandy said.

"Yes, you could put a small branch into the cage and put little ladders up one side and down the other. Grandpa would find you something and you could get the ladders in Walton."

"What a great idea, Mom! We could make it when we get back."

There was a pet shop in Walton where they found just the ladders they wanted. They were made of metal and had hooks at the ends.

"We can hook them over the branch," Mandy said. "He's going to love it, I know."

"Then we could hang something to one end of the branch," James suggested.

"What sort of thing?" Mandy asked.

"How about a couple of wooden thread spools?" Dr. Emily suggested. "They make great hamster toys."

Mandy and James bought one ladder each. Then they bought a new gnawing block, as Frisky had almost bitten his way through his old one. It was important for hamsters to keep their teeth short. Last of all, they bought a bag of special luxury hamster mix.

On the way home, they sat in the back of the car making plans.

"We can set the adventure playground up in Frisky's cage while he's asleep," said Mandy.

"Then it will be a surprise when he wakes up," James said excitedly. "I just can't wait to see what he does!"

"Neither can I," Mandy laughed.

When they got back to Lilac Cottage, Grandpa was outside cleaning the windows. Mandy told him about Frisky's surprise and asked if he would help them.

"Oh, I should think so." Grandpa put down his cloth. "Follow me."

He walked off down the path. "I've had a really busy morning," he told them as they went down to the bottom of the garden. "First the car wouldn't start when Grandma wanted to go shopping. Then just as I got *that* sorted out, John Jenkins came to pick up the things for the sale. Ah . . ."

He stopped under one of the apple trees that grew by the fence. "An apple-tree twig," he said. He took out his penknife and cut one off. "Just the thing for a hamster's adventure playground. What do you think?"

Mandy took it from him. "Great. Thanks, Grandpa."

She suddenly thought of something else. "Do you think Grandma would mind if we looked in her sewing box?"

"What for?" Grandpa asked.

"A couple of empty wooden thread spools," James said. "We're going to hang them from the branch."

"I'm sure she won't mind," Grandpa said. "Make sure you put everything back, though."

"We will." Mandy and James dashed indoors.

Mandy found two thread spools while James found some string in a kitchen drawer. Together they tied them on to the apple-tree twig.

Mandy sat back. "Frisky's going to have a lot of fun with those," she said. "Come on, let's set it up while he's still asleep."

They took everything upstairs. Mandy put her finger to her lips. "Let's be very quiet," she whispered.

She opened the door softly. Then she froze with shock. The table by the radiator was empty. It wasn't only the stuff for the rummage sale that was gone.

Frisky was gone, too!

7

All Locked Up

Mandy and James stood gazing at the empty table. They could hardly believe Frisky had just vanished into thin air.

Then Mandy gave a little laugh of relief. "Grandma must have moved him," she said. "She knew Mr. Jenkins was coming this morning. Maybe she's put Frisky in the living room."

They ran downstairs. Frisky *wasn't* in the living room. They looked in the study, and then through the rest of the house. Frisky was nowhere to be found.

"Let's go and ask your grandpa," James said. They dashed outside.

"Grandpa, where's Frisky?" she called anxiously.

"Frisky? In your room, isn't he?" Grandpa had finished cleaning the windows and was in his gardening shed.

Mandy shook her head. "No, he's gone."

Grandpa tipped his cap to the back of his head and frowned. "Come on, let's take a look."

Mandy and James followed him inside and back upstairs. "He's not there, honestly," Mandy wailed.

"We've looked *everywhere*," James added.

Grandpa stood in the bedroom doorway, his hands on his hips. "Well, I don't know, I'm sure . . ."

Mandy was beginning to feel desperate. Where *could* Frisky have gone?

Then James had an idea.

"Maybe he went with the things for the sale," he said.

Mandy looked at him in horror. "Surely no one would think we were giving Frisky to a rummage sale," she said.

James shrugged. "If he was asleep in his nest, Mr. Jenkins wouldn't have been able to see him, would he?"

Grandpa looked thoughtful. "You know, James is right," he said. "John might have thought it was an empty cage."

"Oh, Grandpa!" Mandy could hardly hold back the tears.

"Come on," Grandpa said. He put his arm around her. "Let's call John."

They went back down the stairs. Grandpa dialed Mr. Jenkins's number, but there was no answer.

"Can't we go to his house?" Mandy asked anxiously. "He might just be out in the garden and not hearing the phone."

Grandpa shook his head. "I'm sorry, Mandy, I don't know where he lives. We'll have to wait until your grandma gets back from the supermarket. She'll know."

"Would he have taken the stuff to his house?" James asked.

Mandy stared at him. Then her face cleared. "No, of *course* not!" she said. "He would have taken it to the village hall. Let's go and see." She rushed off to get her coat.

"But it'll be all locked up," Grandpa called as they ran out. "You should wait till Grandma gets back."

"We'll go and see anyway," Mandy shouted, halfway down the path. "It won't hurt to look."

She couldn't possibly wait until Grandma got back. She might be away for a long time. Mandy had to do something *now*.

Mandy and James raced down the street across the green to the village hall. Jean Knox was just coming out of the general store.

"What's the rush, Mandy?" she called.

Mandy skidded to a halt and quickly told Jean what had happened.

"Oh, dear," Jean said. "I hope you find him all right. Let me know if I can help."

"We will!" James called as they both ran off.

Mr. Hadcroft was putting up an ad on the church bulletin board. Mandy was in such a hurry that she nearly ran into him.

"Hey, hey . . . !" He took hold of her arms. "Where's the fire?"

"We've lost Frisky," Mandy panted. She told him the story.

Mr. Hadcroft patted her shoulder. "Well, try not to worry, Mandy. I'm sure he'll be okay."

"I do hope so." Mandy still felt close to tears.

"If I see John Jenkins, I'll tell him," Mr. Hadcroft called.

"Thanks," Mandy shouted over her shoulder.

They reached the village hall and hurried through the gate and up the steps. Mandy grabbed the door handle. She twisted and pushed. Nothing happened. Grandpa had been right. The hall was all locked up.

James jumped up and down, trying to see through one of the windows. "I can't reach," he panted.

"Here." Mandy tried to lift him up, but he kept slipping out of her grasp.

"It's no use," she panted. "You're too heavy. Can't we find something to stand on?" She looked around desperately.

There was an orange plastic milk crate by the back door. Mandy went to get it. She turned it upside down and stood on it.

"I still can't see," she said. She was standing on tiptoe and the crate was wobbling.

"You'll fall off," James warned.

Mandy got down. She sat on the crate and put her head in her hands. "Oh, James. Poor Frisky. What are we going to do?"

James sat beside her. "Maybe we should go back home and wait for your grandma."

"I'm not leaving until I find out if he's in there!" Mandy said stubbornly.

James sighed. "Okay, but I don't know what good it will do."

Luckily it wasn't long before they saw
Grandma's car coming down the road.

Mandy jumped to her feet. "Grandma!" She
ran to the curb and waved her arms.
"Grandma! Grandma! Stop!"

Grandma pulled up beside her. She wound
down the window. "Mandy, what's wrong?"
she asked anxiously.

Mandy's words all seemed to tumble over
one another as she told Grandma what had
happened.

"Oh, dear." Grandma gave a little chuck. "Poor Frisky. Hop in, you two, I'll take you to John Jenkins's house. He probably has a key." When she saw Mandy's worried face she stopped smiling. "Don't worry, Mandy, I'm sure Frisky will be all right."

"That's what everyone keeps saying," Mandy said. "But it will be cold and damp in the hall and he'll be terrified if he wakes up in a strange place."

Grandma patted her knee. "We'll soon sort this out, don't worry. And he'll be very safe in his cage."

When they reached Mr. Jenkins's house, Grandma knocked at the door, but there was still no answer and the windows were all dark.

Mandy wriggled in her seat. "Oh, James," she said. "What are we going to do now?"

8

Safe and Sound

Grandma came back to the car looking thoughtful. She got in and started the engine.

"We'll have to go and get the key from Mr. Markham," she said.

"Who's he?" James asked as they drove back toward the village center.

"Chairman of the church council," Grandma told them. "I know he's got a key to the hall. I have to get it from him before our meetings."

"I hope *he's* home," Mandy said. "Otherwise I don't know what we're going to do."

They drew up outside Number 2, The Terrace, the home of Mr. Markham.

"You two stay here," Grandma said. "I'll go and see if he's here."

Mandy peered out the car window anxiously. It was getting dark now and a cold wind was blowing. There wouldn't be any heating in the village hall. She felt sick with fear. If Frisky was in there, the cold would be too much for him.

It wasn't long before someone answered the door. Grandma disappeared inside for a minute or two, then came back out waving a key. She hurried down the path and got into the car.

"Here we are," she said briskly. She gave the key to Mandy. "Problem solved."

Grandma drove quickly along the main street to the village hall. She pulled up outside and

Mandy and James jumped out. Mandy un-locked the door and ran inside.

Quickly she turned on the light. The sale things were there. Piles of them. Bags, boxes, even suitcases full of old clothes, all waiting to be sorted through the following morning. Someone had even already put up long tables.

Mandy gave a shiver. It felt freezing, just as she had feared it would. Frisky would be cold and frightened and so bewildered he wouldn't know *where* he was.

But where *was* Frisky? Mandy and James carefully pulled aside bags and boxes, but there wasn't a hamster cage anywhere.

Mandy sat on a chair and burst into tears.

"Don't cry, Mandy," James said. "He's got to be somewhere."

Grandma joined them and put her arm around Mandy.

"Don't upset yourself, darling. Mr. Jenkins must have spotted him and taken him home," Grandma said.

"But Mr. Jenkins isn't *at* home," Mandy sobbed.

Grandma got up. "We'll return Mr. Markham's key, then we'll go and see if John Jenkins is back."

But when they reached Mr. Jenkins's house, it was still in total darkness.

"I'll go next door," Grandma said. "They might know how long he'll be."

When she came back she shook her head. "Sorry, Mandy, he won't be back until late. I'm afraid we'll just have to wait until the morning."

They dropped James off at his gate.

"I'll come early and see what's happened," he said.

"Okay." Mandy sat sadly in the back of the car. She didn't know *how* she was going to get any sleep that night. She would be worrying about Frisky all the time.

When they got home, Grandpa was waiting anxiously.

"Any luck?" he asked as they came in.

Grandma shook her head. "No, I'm afraid not."

Grandpa put his arm around Mandy. "Try not to worry," he said. "He's got a snug nest and plenty of food. He'll be all right."

It seemed really quiet in Mandy's room with no hamster whizzing around on his wheel or tearing in and out of his cardboard roll. His adventure playground still lay on the table where Mandy and James had left it.

About ten o'clock Mandy heard the phone ring and Grandma's voice answering it. Then Grandma came up the stairs. The bedroom door opened.

"Are you asleep, Mandy?"

"No, Grandma," she said. "What's up?"

"John Jenkins has just phoned," Grandma told her.

Mandy sat up quickly. Her heart thudded. "What did he say?" she asked anxiously.

Grandma sat on the bed. "It seems the whole village has found out about Frisky," she said

with a smile. "Jean saw Walter. Walter told Mr.
Hadcroft who said he knew already. Mr. Hadcroft phoned Mr. Markham, who had just
gotten home. Mr. Markham phoned John
and John phoned me." Grandma chuckled.

Mandy wrung her hands together. "But,
Grandma, what about *Frisky*?"

"John's got him at home," Grandma said
with a smile. "He's absolutely fine."

"Oh, thank goodness!" Mandy threw her
arms around her grandma's neck in delight.

Grandma laughed. "Hey, you're strangling me."

Mandy let go. "Sorry, Grandma." Her eyes were shining. "Tell me what happened."

"Wait and see John in the morning," Grandma said. "He's taking Frisky to the hall first thing. I said you and James would go and help them arrange the things for the sale. John can tell you the story himself then."

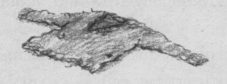

9

None the Worse

The next morning James went to Lilac Cottage bright and early. Mandy was still having breakfast.

"Sit down and have some toast and homemade jam," Grandma said to James when he arrived. "I'll make you a cup of hot chocolate."

"Thanks, Dr. Emily." James sat down next to Mandy. "Have you heard anything about Frisky?" he asked anxiously. "I've been thinking about him all night."

Mandy quickly told him about John's late-night phone call.

"Thank goodness!" James heaped a spoonful of strawberry jam onto his toast. "I hardly slept last night."

"Are you coming to help out today, Tom?" Grandma asked Grandpa.

Grandpa looked up from his gardening magazine. "If you want me to, Dorothy."

"The more the merrier." Grandma began clearing away the dishes. Mandy got up to give her a hand, but she was in such a hurry she almost dropped a plate. Grandma took it from her.

"I can see you're dying to get down to that hall, dear," she said. "Off you go, both of you. We'll come along later."

James snatched up the last of his toast and they headed out the door.

"You've got jam all around your mouth."
Mandy grinned at James as they hurried along
to the hall. She felt on top of the world now
that she knew Frisky was safe and sound. She
just couldn't wait to see him again.

James licked his mouth. He wrinkled up his
nose and looked at Mandy. "Is it off?"

"Yep." Mandy grinned. "Race you!" They
took off down the street, shouting noisily.

When they got there, the hall was full of ac-
tivity. Half a dozen ladies were sorting old
clothes, a teenage girl was in charge of the
tapes and CDs, and Mr. Hadcroft was arrang-
ing a pile of toys.

There was a woman folding up pairs of pants
and putting them in a pile on the table by the
door.

"Can we see Mr. Jenkins, please?" Mandy
panted. She had arrived just seconds before
James.

"He's over by the stage." The woman
pointed. "Sorting the garden tools."

A tall man in a flat cap and tweed jacket was

tying a bunch of battered-looking tools together. As Mandy went up to him, something caught her eye. There, on top of the piano, was Frisky's cage.

Mandy gave a shout and leaped up on the stage. "Frisky!" She had thought he would be fast asleep, but all the hustle and bustle must have woken him up. He was sitting by his food bowl.

Mandy beamed at him through the bars of the cage. "Oh, Frisky, I'm *so* happy to see you! Are you all right?"

Frisky twitched his nose, then went on eating. He looked perfectly well; perky as ever and stuffing his cheek pouches full of food. He seemed the same as ever after his journey around Welford.

"He's fine," a deep voice said behind her. "You must be Mandy?"

Mandy turned to see Mr. Jenkins smiling at her.

"Oh, Mr. Jenkins," said Mandy. "I've been so worried about him."

"I know," Mr. Jenkins said. "I'm really sorry. When I picked up the sale things I thought the cage was empty."

"I thought that's what had happened." James put his finger through the bars to tickle Frisky under the chin.

"People give all sorts of things to rummage sales. I just thought maybe someone had lost a hamster and was giving away the cage."

"It doesn't matter," Mandy said. "He's safe and sound, that's the important thing."

"When did you find him?" James asked.

"I was unloading all the stuff," Mr. Jenkins told them. "And I was just going to lock up when I heard a strange noise. I'll tell you, it gave me quite a scare."

Mandy frowned. "What do you mean?"

"Well," Mr. Jenkins raised his eyebrows. "It was a squeak, squeak . . . I thought it was a ghost!"

Mandy and James burst out laughing.

Mr. Jenkins was laughing, too.

"What did you do?" Mandy asked.

"Well, I tracked the noise down to a pile of old curtains," Mr. Jenkins said. "Then, when I moved them aside, there was the hamster cage with this little fellow running inside his wheel like a maniac. I was mighty relieved, I can tell you."

"I bet," James said.

"I was going to phone your grandma," Mr. Jenkins said. "But I'd promised my wife I'd take her to the movies in Walton, and she was all ready to go when I got back. I'm sorry you were so worried, Mandy."

"It's okay." Mandy beamed him a smile. "As long as he's all right. He's not mine, you see. I've been looking after him for Grandma's friend. He's been staying at Hamster Hotel."

It was Mr. Jenkins's turn to look surprised. "Hamster Hotel?"

James chuckled. "Lilac Cottage," he explained.

"Oh," said Mr. Jenkins. "I see." He looked rather puzzled and Mandy didn't really think he saw at all.

Grandma and Grandpa arrived. They came to see Frisky, then left to help prepare for the sale.

"Do you want to give me a hand?" Grandma asked Mandy. "You could help Grandpa with the books and magazines if you like, James."

"Sure," James said.

"If there's a book on dog training, you'd better buy it, James," Mandy called as she went to help Grandma.

"Good idea." James began hunting through the pile.

Grandma was sorting through a heap of old sweaters and jackets.

"Hey." Mandy picked one up. "This looks like Grandpa's old —"

But she got no further. Grandma had snatched the sweater from her fingers. "Shh. He doesn't know," she whispered.

But it was too late. Grandpa had seen it. He came rushing over faster than Mandy had ever seen him move before.

"Dorothy!" His voice was like thunder.

Grandma was holding the sweater behind her back. "Yes, dear?" she said calmly.

"Dorothy!" Grandpa was running around, trying to see behind her back. "That looks like . . . "

Everyone had stopped work to watch.

"It is, Mr. Hope," James called. "It's your gardening sweater." Then his hand flew to his mouth. He had let the cat out of the bag.

Grandpa held out his hand toward Grandma.

"Thank you, James. I'm glad we men stick together. Give it to me, Dorothy," he ordered sternly.

"It's full of holes," Grandma said.

"I like them." Grandpa was still holding out his hand.

"It's faded," Grandma said.

"I like it faded." Grandpa tried to grab the sweater.

"It . . . it . . . smells!" Grandma backed away.

"I'll wash it," Grandpa promised. "Anyway, it's a nice smell. Earthy . . . "

"It's, it's . . . " Grandma couldn't think of anything else.

". . . it's Grandpa's favorite sweater," Mandy finished for her.

"Oh, well, all right." Grandma gave it to Grandpa with a sigh. Everyone laughed and clapped.

Then Grandma laughed, too. She put her arms around Grandpa and gave him a hug. "Oh, Tom, you'll be the death of me," she said, wiping her eyes.

"Nonsense." Grandpa gave her a loud kiss on the cheek.

"I've been looking for my sweater everywhere," Grandpa said to Mandy when Grandma had gone back to sorting clothes. "I might have known your grandma would try to pull a trick like that."

Mandy suddenly remembered how Grandpa had spent ages looking through all the drawers and closets. So that's what he had been up to. She laughed and gave him a hug.

"Is it all right if we take Frisky home now?" Mandy asked Grandpa when all the things were sorted neatly into piles on the tables. It was almost lunchtime.

Grandpa looked at his watch. "Yes. I'll take you home if you like. We don't want Frisky out in that cold air. We'll come back later for the sale." He glanced over to where Grandma was talking to two of the ladies. "Who knows, I might even find myself another sweater with holes in it."

Mandy and James laughed. They said good-bye to everyone and put Frisky carefully in the car. Frisky hadn't been at all worried by the noise and bustle and had gone into his nest for a snooze.

Mandy felt excited as they traveled back to Lilac Cottage.

She just couldn't wait to show Frisky his adventure playground!

10

Farewell

On the way home they passed Dr. Adam coming out of Animal Ark.

"Please stop, Grandpa," Mandy said. "I *must* tell Dad about Frisky."

Grandpa pulled up and she rolled down her window.

Dr. Adam laughed as he listened to her story.

"I don't know, Mandy," he said. "You do get into some crazy situations."

"It wasn't *my* fault," Mandy said. "We've given Frisky the best care in the world."

"I know, Mandy," her dad said. "Well, we'll be happy to have you back home. It's been really quiet without you," he added, teasing her.

"Is my bedroom finished?" Mandy asked. She had been looking forward to seeing it now that it had been decorated.

"Yep." Dr. Adam opened the door of his car and put his bag inside. "It looks great. Great color, although I think you'll have all your posters up again and we won't be able to see much of the walls."

"I sure will. See you later, Dad." Mandy rolled the window up. "I'll have to get one of a hamster to remind me of Frisky," she said to James and Grandpa.

"Me, too," James said. "That's if I can find enough space on my wall."

Dr. Adam waved as they drove away toward Lilac Cottage.

Back indoors, they took Frisky up to the spare room.

"Here we are." Mandy put the cage on the table. "Home, safe and sound."

James peered into the cage. "You know, I don't think he really cares where he is as long as he's got a nice warm nest to curl up in."

"I bet he didn't like that cold old hall." Mandy picked up the little apple-tree branch. "Come on, let's make his playground while he's asleep."

Mandy and James carefully fixed the branch inside the cage. They hung the thread spools from one end.

"If we tie them together, he'll be able to jump over them," Mandy said.

They did that, then they put the ladders into position. Last of all they thoroughly cleaned out the cage and filled Frisky's food bowl and water bottle.

"There," Mandy said when they had finished. "All clean for tomorrow."

"Tomorrow?" James said.

"He's going home," Mandy told him sadly.

"Oh," said James. "Our vacation's over, then. We haven't done much training with Blackie, have we?"

"Not really," Mandy said. "We could do some this afternoon if you like."

James bit his lip. "I think I'd rather help out at the rummage sale."

Mandy grinned. "Me, too."

The following day, Mandy woke up to a strange noise. She sat up, stretched, and yawned. She had oiled Frisky's wheel again, so she knew that couldn't have caused the noise.

Then she saw what it was. Frisky was racing up and down his ladders, along his apple branch, and over and over his thread spools. He was having the time of his life.

Mandy gave a little cry of delight and jumped out of bed. She sat and watched him race around and around. Eventually he stopped and took a drink from his water bottle. Then he sat washing his face. After that he just stared

at Mandy for a minute or two, his little nose twitching. It was almost as if he was saying "thank you."

Mandy waggled her finger through the bars.

"Now you behave yourself when you get back home," she said. She opened the cage door and picked him up. He ran up her arm, then sat on her shoulder. Mandy could see him in the mirror. He looked so bright and perky. She felt proud that she and James had looked after him so well.

She let Frisky run around for a while, and then put him back in his cage. "I've got to pack my bag, Frisky," she told him. "I'm going home today, too."

Mandy dressed and packed her bag. She took it downstairs. Grandma and Grandpa were sitting at the kitchen table.

"You're going home today?" Grandpa looked up from the Sunday paper.

"Yes." Mandy sat down and helped herself to some cereal. "I'm really going to miss Frisky."

"He'll miss you, too, I'm sure," Grandma said. She was counting the money taken in at the rummage sale. "I don't suppose he's ever had so much luxury."

Mandy smiled. "He loves his adventure playground."

"Good," Grandma said. "It'll be something for him to remember his vacation by."

"That's what we thought." Mandy still sounded sad.

Grandpa folded up his paper. "Well, I'd better go and dig up those potatoes for lunch. You staying for lunch, Mandy?"

Mandy bit her lip. She *wanted* to stay with Frisky as long as possible but she wanted to get home, too. She was beginning to miss it, and she was dying to see her bedroom.

Grandma sat back, looking pleased. "Over five hundred dollars!" she said. "That'll help with the funds for the new church roof." She looked at Grandpa over the top of her glasses. "There would have been more if you'd have let me sell your sweater, Tom."

Grandpa gave a grunt and fumbled in his pocket. He took out a few bills and gave them to Grandma. "Oh, here you are, then." His eyes twinkled.

Grandma took them and put them in the bag with the rest of the money. "Thanks, Tom."

"When is Frisky's owner coming for him?" Mandy asked.

"This morning," Grandma said. "They actually got back late last night, so I should think she'll be here quite soon."

"I bet she missed Frisky," Mandy said.

"I'm sure she did. But she'll be so pleased he's been taken care of so well." Grandma put her arm around Mandy. "I'm really grateful for your help, Mandy."

"It's okay, Grandma."

Mandy suddenly thought of all the things she had to do that day. She had promised to go for a walk with James and Blackie. She wanted to put her books back into their bookcase and stick her posters back up on her bedroom wall. And she and James were going to read the dog training book James had bought at the sale. It might have some helpful hints on what to do with Blackie.

Mandy looked at her grandma. "Would it be all right if I went home after breakfast?"

"Of course it would," Grandma said. "Go when you like. You know you can come back any time."

"Thanks, Grandma." Mandy quickly finished her toast, then went upstairs again. Frisky was sitting on his branch. He looked slightly sleepy now.

Mandy peered through the bars. "Bye, Frisky." There was a little catch in her voice. "I hope you've enjoyed your vacation." She took him out for one last time and stroked him gently. Then, seeing how sleepy he was, she put him carefully back inside. He scrambled up to his little platform, turned, and gazed at her for a minute. His whiskers twitched. Then he climbed into his nest. Soon all Mandy could see was a tight little ball of fur.

Outside, the early morning mist had cleared

and the sun was shining. It was going to be a lovely autumn day. Mandy ran down the hill and along past the green. The front door of Animal Ark was open and Dr. Emily was just coming out.

"Mom!" Mandy shouted and ran up the path to meet her.

Dr. Emily gave her a hug. "Mandy! I was just going to walk up to the cottage to meet you."

"I couldn't wait to get back," said Mandy. "How's everything? How's the chinchilla?"

"He's fine. Everything's fine."

Mandy and her mom went inside. The smell of fresh paint greeted Mandy as she ran up the stairs and burst in through her bedroom door. She drew in her breath. It looked beautiful. Clean and fresh and bright.

Mandy sat on her bed. She thought about Frisky, all curled up snug in his little nest. She hoped he would be happy to be going home, too.

Just then her mom called from the bottom of the stairs. "Mandy, we've got a badger cub someone's brought in. Come down and see him."

Mandy leaped up. How wonderful! She had never seen a badger cub close up. She ran downstairs to join her mom.

There was no doubt about it. It had been fun staying at Hamster Hotel, but Animal Ark was the best!